the **nativity** story™

NEW LINE CINEMA PRESENTS A TEMPLE HILL PRODUCTION "THE NATIVITY STORY" KEISHA CASTLE-HUGHES OSCAR ISAAC HIAM ABBASS SHAUN TOUB ALEXANDER SIDDIG WITH CIARAN HINDS AND SHOHREH AGHDASHLOO CASTING BY MINDY MARIN MUSIC BY MYCHAEL DANNA COSTUME DESIGN BY MAURIZIO MILLENOTTI EDITED BY ROBERT K. LAMBERT, A.C.E. STUART LEVY, A.C.E. PRODUCTION DESIGN BY STEFANO MARIA ORTOLANI DIRECTOR OF PHOTOGRAPHY ELLIOT DAVIS EXECUTIVE PRODUCERS TOBY EMMERICH CALE BOYTER MIKE RICH CATHERINE HARDWICKE TIM VAN RELLIM PRODUCED BY WYCK GODFREY MARTY BOWEN WRITTEN BY MIKE RICH DIRECTED BY CATHERINE HARDWICKE

www.thenativitystory.com   NEW LINE CINEMA

HarperCollins®, 🅜®, and HarperEntertainment™ are trademarks of HarperCollins Publishers.

The Nativity Story: Children's Movie Storybook
Printed in the United States of America.
All rights reserved. No part of this book may be used or reproduced in any manner whatsoever without
written permission except in the case of brief quotations embodied in critical articles and reviews.
For information address HarperCollins Children's Books, a division of HarperCollins Publishers,
1350 Avenue of the Americas, New York, NY 10019.
Library of Congress catalog card number: 2006934339.
ISBN-10: 0-06-128522-6 — ISBN-13: 978-0-06-128522-6
Typography by Patrick Collins
1 3 5 7 9 10 8 6 4 2
❖
First Edition
www.harpercollinschildrens.com

the nativity story
CHILDREN'S MOVIE STORYBOOK

Adapted by SADIE CHESTERFIELD

Photographs by JAIMIE TRUEBLOOD

HarperEntertainment

An Imprint of HarperCollinsPublishers

There was trouble in the town of Nazareth. King Herod's soldiers arrived on horseback. They were there to deliver bad news. All of the townspeople would have to return to the place their family had come from—no matter how far away that was.

In a small house, a family discussed Herod's orders. Mary was the oldest daughter of Anna and Joaquim.

She was pregnant with her first child. But this child was unlike any other.

Months before, something strange had happened. Mary was alone in an olive grove. An angel named Gabriel visited her. He told her she would bear the son of God. Her son would be the Messiah, or Savior. He would free the Jews from King Herod's rule. Joseph, Mary's husband, could not believe it. A child by the Holy Spirit? How could that be? But one night, in a dream, he too was visited by Gabriel. Now Mary and Joseph were united under God.

Joseph turned to his new family. He was worried. "The order was for each man to go to the place of his ancestors," he said. "I must go to Bethlehem."

Anna was scared for her daughter. Mary was Joseph's family now. She would have to go with him. But the baby would arrive soon—traveling would be hard on Mary.

"The journey to Bethlehem is more than a hundred miles," Anna said. Mary was afraid too. But she knew she could not stay in Nazareth. If she did, she would have to face Herod's soldiers.

"I am going with my husband," she told her mother.

"I pray you are hearing God's will better than I," Anna replied.

And so it was. Mary and Joseph set out for Bethlehem. Joseph led the donkey through the wide, open plains.

Mary and Joseph were not the only ones starting a long journey. Three wise men named Melchior, Gaspar, and Balthasar had been watching a star move across the sky. Soon it would align with the planets. It would create the most spectacular sight. This was told to happen *only* with the coming of the Savior. The three Magi would travel across deserts and mountains. They would follow this star to the holy child.

Gaspar was looking at the sky doubtfully. Melchior turned to him.

"The star we follow speaks of a king. His mother. His father. Still you speak of these writings, this star, as nothing more than foolish musings." It was true. Even though they had come far, Gaspar was not certain of their journey.

"If this star is God's way of proclaiming a new Messiah, he is doing so quietly," Gaspar replied.

In small towns everywhere there was word of the new king. Mary and Joseph made their way through Ginaea. They heard a preacher on the corner crying out, "Behold, your king is coming to you! His dominion will be from sea to sea and from the river to the ends of the earth."

Children danced and laughed in the street. A woman selling ribbons saw Mary passing by. She pulled the most beautiful ribbon from its spool. She gave it to Mary as a gift.

There was no celebrating in the royal palace. When King Herod heard the prophecy, he was angry.

"Judea. Samaria. Galilee. All of them talk of this king, this man who will defeat me." Antipas, King Herod's son, tried to comfort his father. It was no use. King Herod stormed on. "I have had a wife betray me. I have had two sons do the same. Where are they now?"

Antipas looked serious. "They are no more," he said quietly.

King Herod knew what he had to do. "I will end this threat to my rule. As I have all threats."

Mary and Joseph continued on their journey. The roads were more dangerous, the hills steeper, the miles longer. Joseph's feet were cracked and bloody. He had been walking too long in the heat. There was little food left. Joseph wondered how much longer their tired donkey would last. As Mary slept, Joseph looked out into the night sky. He was worried. He was afraid. "If I am doing your will, I pray you give me a sign," he said softly. But there was no response.

The following day things got worse. While crossing the river, Mary and Joseph were washed downstream. They struggled in the rapids. Finally they grabbed hold of a fallen tree limb. They barely made it out alive.

The Magi's caravan made its way down a Jerusalem street. The Magi caught the eye of a few townspeople... and one of Herod's soldiers. He took the wise men to the palace. King Herod was waiting for them. Melchior explained, "Your Excellency, I have waited a lifetime for the signs I've now seen."

Balthasar told King Herod of the prophecy, and of
the star they had been following for months.

King Herod had an idea. "I too have been waiting for
God's king," he said with a smile. "Go to Bethlehem
and search for this child. And when you've found him,
return . . . so that I may come worship him as well."

Mary and Joseph traveled down the road north of Bethlehem. Mary shivered. She wrapped her blanket tightly around herself.

"Your woman is cold," a voice called from the darkness. An old shepherd sat in front of a fire. Mary and Joseph joined him. The old shepherd looked at Mary's stomach. "My father told me long ago that we are all given something. A gift. Your gift is what you carry inside."

"What was your gift?" Mary asked.

"Nothing," the old shepherd said. "Nothing but the hope of waiting for one."

Joseph stood and thanked the shepherd. He pulled his young wife to her feet. They would have to leave now. They needed to make it to Bethlehem by morning.

The tired donkey plodded along. Mary rested her head on the animal's neck. Suddenly she cried out in pain. Joseph pulled the donkey into a run. They were right outside of Bethlehem. "We will find a place, I promise," Joseph assured his wife. "There will be many to help us." But there was no one to help them. As Joseph ran from house to house he was met with shaking heads. "Please," Joseph begged. But no one would let them inside. Mary began to weep. She begged God to help them.

Joseph pounded on yet another door. "Please," he repeated, "my wife is near birth. There is no one to help us. I ask not of your house, but anyplace you have." The old man looked out at Mary. He could tell she was in pain. He led Mary and Joseph around the back of the house.

"It is all I can do," he said. Joseph stared at the structure before him. There stood a small, humble stable.

Mary lay down on the stable floor. The pain was more intense than ever. She held the red ribbon in her clenched fist. Joseph tried to comfort her. Overhead, a star was moving toward two planets—Venus and Jupiter.

As Mary gave one final gasp, the star fell into align-ment with the planets. The night sky was filled with light. The baby cried out. Joseph placed the child on Mary's tattered clothing. The couple wept sweet, silent tears of relief. The Savior was born.

On an old road south of Jerusalem, the Magi looked up in awe. The light from the star brightened their faces. This was the most amazing event in three thousand years. Melchior couldn't help but smile. "How is your faith now?" he asked the doubting Gaspar.

The old shepherd had his eyes locked on the star as well . . . until the angel Gabriel appeared. Gabriel told the shepherd that the Savior had been born. He told him to find the child in a manger. Then he disappeared.

The old shepherd climbed to the top of the hill. He saw the most glorious sight. All over Bethlehem, other shepherds had their eyes on the star. They too had seen Gabriel. They too had heard the message from God. And so they set off to find the child—the Savior who was born and then placed in a humble manger.

The old shepherd entered the stable first. He saw a familiar face—Mary's. The mother of his Lord was the same woman who had sat by his fire. He smiled and reached his hand toward the child. But he drew it back suddenly. Mary reassured him, "He is for all mankind." The old shepherd placed his hand on the child. A tear rolled down his cheek. "We are all given a gift," Mary said softly.

On a road nearby, the Magi's caravan came to a stop. Far beneath the bright star the wise men saw a stable. Even from the roadside they could see the shepherds, Joseph, Mary, and the child. All were covered in starlight. Melchior was overcome. "The greatest of kings, born in the most humble of places," he said.

The three wise men were moved by the scene. As they approached Mary and her child, they dropped to their knees . . . even Gaspar. Humbly, they presented gifts covered with fine linen.

"A gift of gold, for the king of kings," Melchior said.

"Frankincense," Balthasar offered, "for the priest of all priests."

"A gift of myrrh to honor thy sacrifice," Gaspar added.

That night the child named Jesus slept soundly. He was loved. He was adored. He was king.

The next morning the star still shone brightly at dawn. Joseph looked at his wife and child. The three of them were alone now. "Are you well?" he asked. Mary smiled. She was more certain of her faith than ever.

The Magi's caravan came to a stop at the road to Jerusalem. It was time to tell King Herod the heavenly news. But the Magi did not move. Glancing at one another, they continued on their journey. The road to Jerusalem disappeared in the dust.

King Herod stared out his window. He was looking for signs of the wise men. "It has been three days now," he said. "They have sent no word." The king lashed out at his son before he could argue. "And do not tell me they may still return! These men will not come back."

"There are shepherds in Judea telling everyone of a child born in Bethlehem," the king continued.

"They are only shepherds, Your Excellency," Herod's soldier Phasael said.

"They are a voice I do not need to hear. This child . . . did they say when he was born?"

"They made no such claim," Antipas replied.

"Send your soldiers to this town . . . and find every young boy there. Every boy under two years . . .

"Spare no one," King Herod finished. "If a young king has indeed been born in Bethlehem, he will also die there."

Herod's soldiers climbed onto their horses. They lit their torches and headed for Bethlehem. They would carry out the orders of the king. They would find the child—the Messiah.

Joseph, Mary, and Jesus rested in the stable. Suddenly a violent dream woke Joseph from sleep. God was sending him a sign—Joseph's family was in danger. Joseph prepared the donkey for the journey out of Bethlehem. He looked at his young wife and child. There was little time.

Storm clouds gathered in the sky. A roll of thunder sounded in the air. King Herod waited silently in the palace. "The prophecy will end tonight, Father. The sons of Bethlehem shall be no more," Antipas assured him.

Phasael led the small army into town. Their torches remained lit despite the heavy rain. "All soldiers," he called out, "carry out the orders of King Herod!"

The soldiers dismounted and the attack began. Fists pounded on doors, swords were pulled from their sheaths, and villagers were called from their houses. The air was filled with shouts and screams. The soldiers forced their way into homes. They pulled small children from their mothers' arms.

A lone soldier was heading into town. Suddenly something caught his eye—the stable. He rode toward it. He entered the stable and crept toward the manger. He pulled his sword from its sheath. Silently, he stabbed the wood with the sword. He tilted the manger toward him to find . . . nothing. He kicked over the manger with an angry grunt.

In the desert outside of Bethlehem, Joseph and his family were making their escape. The road ahead was long, but the rain had stopped. The stars now shone brightly above their heads. Off in the distance, a familiar voice sounded. It was Gabriel. "Arise, Joseph; take the child and his mother and flee to Egypt. And remain there until I bring you word." Joseph looked at Mary. The couple looked down at their new baby. They shared a smile. They would travel to Egypt. They would wait for Gabriel. They would not be afraid.